Chicken Little

Retold & illustrated by
STEVEN KELLOGG

HarperCollins*Publishers*

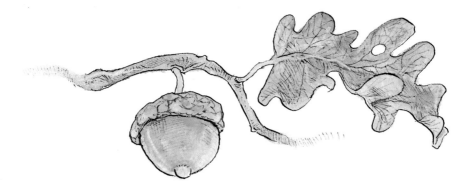

To Colin, with love

Chicken Little
Copyright © 1985 by Steven Kellogg
Printed in Hong Kong. All rights reserved.

Library of Congress Cataloging-in-Publication Data
Kellogg, Steven.
  Chicken little / by Steven Kellogg.
      p.   cm.
  Summary: Chicken Little and his feathered friends, alarmed that the sky seems to be falling, are easy prey to hungry Foxy Loxy when he poses as a police officer in hopes of tricking them into his truck.
  ISBN 0-688-07045-0
  1. Children's stories, American.   [1. Foxes—Fiction.   2. Animals—Fiction.]
I. Title.
PZ7.K292Ch   1985
[E]
                                                                                              84-25519
                                                                                                   CIP
                                                                                                    AC

"Poultry coming," announced Foxy Loxy, as he spotted Chicken Little skipping down the road.

"That little featherhead will make a tasty chicken-salad sandwich," he chuckled.

But before Chicken Little got close enough for Foxy Loxy to pounce, an acorn fell from an oak tree and hit her on the head.

"Help! Help! The sky is falling!" shrieked the little bird.

Her cries were heard by Henny Penny.
"What's the matter?" she asked.

"The sky is falling!" cried Chicken Little. "A piece of it hit
me on the head."

Henny Penny was horrified.

"Call the police!" she cried. "The sky is falling!
The sky is falling!"

"That hen has a plump pair of drumsticks," observed
Foxy Loxy, "and they'll be mighty tasty southern-fried."
He was about to charge forward and capture the two
chickens when the clamor reached Ducky Lucky.

"What's all this cackling about?" he demanded.

"The sky is falling!" cried Henny Penny. "A piece of it hit Chicken Little on the head."

"This is terrible!" squawked Ducky Lucky. And together the three birds wailed: "Help! Police! The sky is falling!"

Foxy Loxy shivered with greed when he imagined how
delicious Ducky Lucky would taste simmered in spices and sauce.

But before he could spring from his hiding place, the cries
of the group were heard by Goosey Lucy and Gosling Gilbert.

"What luck!" whispered the fox. "I'll toast the bite-sized one as soon as I get home, and I'll pop the fat one into the freezer until Christmas."

Foxy Loxy almost fainted with delight when Turkey Lurkey came running across the fields.

"There's my Thanksgiving feast!" he chuckled. "This is the luckiest day of my life."

He was about to pounce on his victims when suddenly he realized it was six against one. "And that turkey and goose look like pretty tough birds," he murmured.

"I'll avoid a scuffle by outsmarting those foolish fowl."

Disguising his truck and himself, he approached the group and announced: "Officer Loxy at your service, folks. What seems to be the problem?"

"The sky is falling!" chorused the birds.
"A piece of it hit me on the head!" added Chicken Little.

"This *is* an emergency!" declared the fox. "Into the truck, and I'll take you directly to headquarters!"

Suddenly, as she looked more closely at the fox, Chicken Little remembered the wanted poster she had seen in town.

"It's Foxy Loxy!" she shrieked. "Run for your lives!"

The birds tried to escape, but Foxy Loxy threw Chicken Little into the truck and locked the door.

Before driving off, the fox couldn't resist reading the recipes he had selected for each of his captives.

"And as for that nonsense about the sky falling," he sneered, "this is what beaned the dim-witted chick!"

With a triumphant laugh he hurled the acorn skyward,
jumped into the truck, and cried, "On to the kitchen!"

The acorn soared above the treetops and lodged itself in the propeller gears of a sky patrol helicopter piloted by Sergeant Hippo Hefty.

The gears jammed, the propeller stopped turning,
and the helicopter plunged toward the earth.

The falling helicopter crashed into the cab of the poultry truck. Foxy Loxy leaped from the wreckage screaming, "THE SKY IS FALLING!   THE SKY IS FALLING!"

"Stop that thug!" cried the birds.

Sergeant Hefty flattened the fleeing fox.
"You're under arrest!" he announced.

"You mean I'm under a fat hippo," snapped Foxy Loxy.

During his trial, Foxy Loxy insisted that he was innocent.
But the judge sent him to prison on a diet of green-bean gruel
and weed juice.

On her way home, Chicken Little recovered the acorn.

She planted it next to her coop.

Years later, when the acorn had grown into an oak tree,
her grandchildren loved to snuggle beside Chicken Little
and listen to her adventure.